Disney Junior

Spidey Saves the Day

Adapted by
Steve Behling

Based on the episodes
"Spidey Surprise": **Baljeet Rai**
"Monkeying Around!": **Ken Kristensen**
"A Helping of Hulk": **Baljeet Rai**
"Lost and Found": **Henry Gifford**
"Attack of the Green Giggles!": **Henry Gifford**

Designed by
David Roe

Los Angeles • New York

Contents

MARVEL
SPIDEY
and his AMAZING FRIENDS

Spidey Surprise

THWIP!

Here comes Spidey.

Oh, no!

It is Green Goblin!
"Welcome to my party,"
he says.

Green Goblin throws
pumpkin pranks.

The pumpkin prank makes
a loud noise.
Spidey throws it away!

Spidey tries to stop
Green Goblin.
But he is out of web-fluid!

Green Goblin flies off
to make more trouble.

Spidey has an idea.
He calls his friend
TRACE-E.

Maybe TRACE-E can bring
Spidey more web-fluid.
But where is it?

TRACE-E needs to find
the box with the web-fluid!

TRACE-E looks in a box.
She finds no web-fluid.

Stop playing, TRACE-E.
Spidey needs your help.

Spidey jumps away from Goblin.
He really needs some webs!

At last, TRACE-E finds
the web-fluid!

TRACE-E will take
the web-fluid to Spidey.

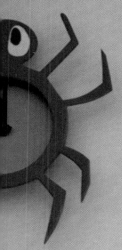

"Which pumpkin shall we play with next?" Goblin asks.

Spidey does not
want to play.

TRACE-E is here!

She gives the web-fluid
to Spidey.

But something is wrong.
The web-fluid
makes confetti!

Green Goblin giggles.
He flies away.

This is not the right web-fluid.
But that is okay!

Spidey will make it work!
TRACE-E gives more
web-fluid to Spidey.

Spidey thwips a web
at Goblin.
It tickles Goblin's nose!

"Hey!" Goblin says.
"Not funny!"

Spidey winks at TRACE-E.
He is going to have
some fun!

TRACE-E gives Spidey
more web-fluid.

THWIP!

Spidey makes web-balloons.

But Goblin gets carried away
by a balloon!

Spidey catches Goblin
with a web.

Spidey wraps up Goblin
like a present.
The day is saved!

Monkeying Around!

There is trouble
at the zoo!
Spidey will help.

Spidey's friend Ms. Marvel
will help, too.

Ms. Marvel can stretch. She can make her hands very big!

Three monkeys are loose.
Spidey and Ms. Marvel
chase the first monkey!

"Where did he go?"
asks Ms. Marvel.

The monkey lands next
to the heroes.
"Eek eek!" says the monkey.

"Come here!" Spidey says.
The monkey leaps
onto a scooter.

The second monkey
grabs some balloons.

It pops them!

The third monkey
tangles up the swing.
Now no one can use it.

The first monkey
crashes into a sandbox.

The monkey pours
out some sand.
It makes a big mess!

Spidey tries to stop them.
But a monkey sprays
Spidey with water!

Spidey thwips a web.
He turns off the water.

A monkey throws a ball
at Ms. Marvel.

The monkey throws more
balls from the playground.

Spidey and Ms. Marvel
will catch the monkey.

But the other monkeys
get in a truck.

The truck starts to roll!
It is rolling toward
the fountain!

Spidey thwips webs
to stop the truck.

But the truck turns sideways!
Can Ms. Marvel stop it?

Yes, she can!

She makes her hands big
and stops the truck.

Spidey thwips a web.
But the monkeys are
too fast for him!

Ms. Marvel tries to catch
the monkeys with her arms.
But she gets all tangled up.

Spidey sees a fruit cart.
He gets an idea!

Spidey buys some
fresh bananas.

Ms. Marvel throws
the bananas
to the monkeys.

Spidey thwips a web net.
The monkeys land on it.
They are happy
eating bananas!

Way to go, Spidey and Ms. Marvel!

A Helping of Hulk

WHOOSH!
Spidey lands on a roof.
Doc Ock must be here.

Doc Ock has an alarm.
How will Spidey get in?

Spidey hears a sound.

It is Hulk!
"What are you doing here?"
Spidey asks.

Hulk wants to help stop Doc Ock.

Spidey says they
must be quiet.

Hulk says he can tiptoe!

Spidey sneaks in on a web.
He does not set off
the alarm!

Hulk tries to sneak in.
SNAP!
He is so big, the web breaks!

Spidey saves Hulk
with a web.

Hulk bounces!

Hulk lands on his feet.
Where is Doc Ock?

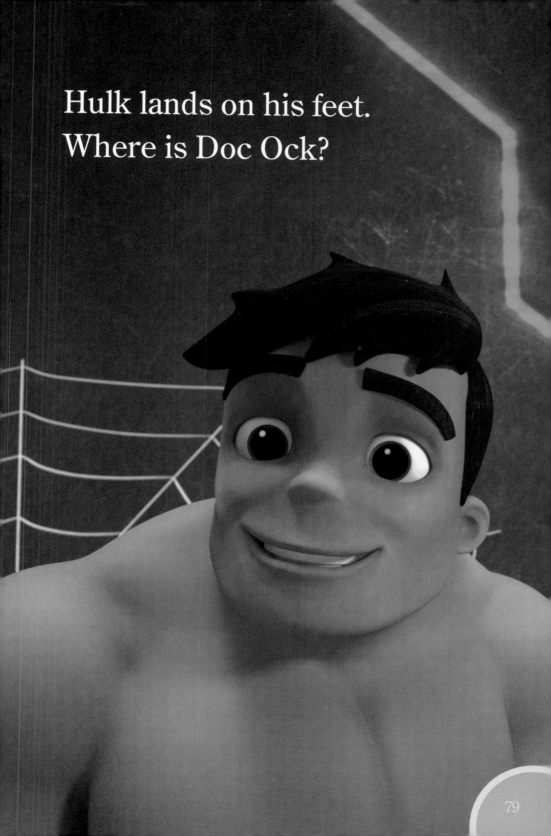

Doc Ock is not here.
But her Octo-Bots are!

Hulk wants to smash.

But Spidey says to wait.

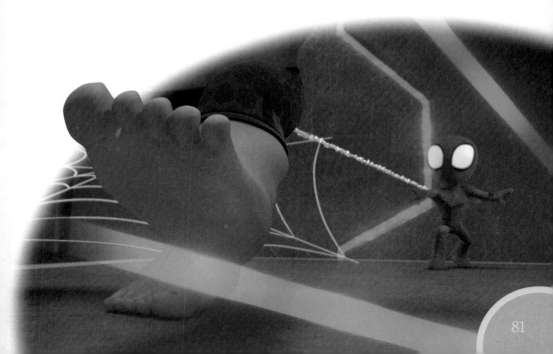

They don't want to
wake up the Octo-Bots.
Spidey will sneak over.

Spidey jumps and flips
past the lasers.

Spidey finds the controls
for the Octo-Bots.

He wipes off some dust.

The dust tickles Hulk's nose.

Hulk sneezes!

Hulk flies across the room.
Spidey catches him.

Spidey touches a laser.
He sets off the alarm!

Doc Ock appears on a screen.
She orders the Octo-Bots
to attack!

Spidey has Spidey-sense.
It warns him of trouble.

The Octo-Bots trap Spidey!

Spidey thwips his webs.
He stops the Octo-Bots!

But the Octo-Bots escape!

The Octo-Bots join together.
They become one
big Octo-Bot.

Spidey asks Hulk for help.

Now is the time to smash!

Hulk picks up the Octo-Bot.

Spidey turns it off!

The heroes stop Doc Ock.
That makes her mad!

Spidey thanks Hulk.
Hulk sure is a big help!

Lost and Found

"Hey, TRACE-E!" Spidey says.
"Want to help me test
my new web-fluid?"

Spidey shoots his web.

It makes a big ball.

TRACE-E's alarm rings.
It is time to meet Aunt May.

Aunt May got tickets
to see a movie.

Spidey puts the tickets
in his backpack.

TRACE-E jumps
in the backpack.

Spidey sees people running.
They are running
from Rhino!

Spidey webs his backpack
to a recycling bin.
"Stay here, TRACE-E!"
he says.

"What are you up to now, Rhino?" Spidey says.

"Seeing how fast I can stomp," Rhino says.

A garbage truck
takes the recycling bin.
It has Peter's backpack!

Spidey thinks he can stop
Rhino *and* get his backpack.

Meanwhile, Rhino
stomps away.

He takes an apple
from a boy!

Rhino almost eats the apple.
But a web yanks
the apple away!

Spidey gives the apple
back to the boy.

Then Spidey swings
after the backpack.

But Rhino makes more trouble.
He tosses cars everywhere!

Spidey catches the cars.

"You won't stop me!"
Rhino says.

He throws a garbage
can lid at Spidey.

Spidey leaps out of the way.

Spidey thwips web blobs.
Rhino is stuck!

Spidey leaves
to get TRACE-E.

Rhino escapes!

The garbage truck drives by.
TRACE-E waves at Spidey!

Rhino knows the backpack
must be special.

Rhino gets to
the backpack first.

Spidey tricks Rhino
into opening the backpack.

TRACE-E gives Rhino
the new web-fluid.

The web-fluid can goes
WHOOSH!
Rhino is trapped in
a big ball of webs!

Spidey saves TRACE-E
and the movie tickets!

Spidey swings to the theater
and changes to Peter.
It's movie time!

Attack of the Green Giggles!

Peter and Aunt May
go to the park.

Peter takes a picture.

The picture is blurry.
Aunt May tells Peter
to keep trying.

Peter hears something.
People are laughing!

It is Green Goblin!
His Giggle Gas
makes everyone laugh.

Peter turns into Spidey.
He will stop Green Goblin!

Giggle Gas is everywhere.

What will Spidey do?

Ms. Marvel appears.
"Maybe I can help!" she says.

Ms. Marvel makes
her hands really big.
She waves the Giggle Gas away!

The heroes chase
Green Goblin.

Spidey uses webs
to stop the Giggle Gas.

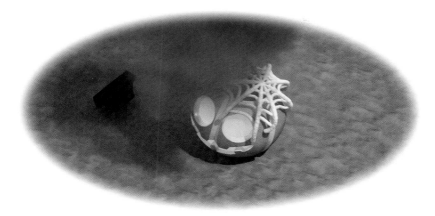

Ms. Marvel waves her hands
to remove the Giggle Gas.

Now Green Goblin
wants ice cream!

The Giggle Gas
makes the driver laugh.

The truck rolls away!

THWIP!

Spidey webs the truck.

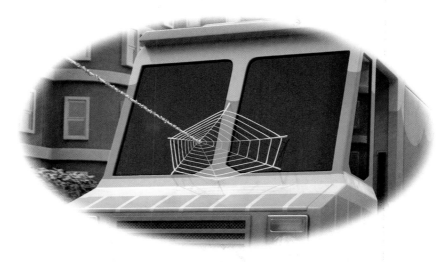

Ms. Marvel grabs the truck.

Now Green Goblin
robs a store.
"Not so fast!" Spidey says.

Green Goblin tries to run.
But Ms. Marvel blocks him!

Green Goblin throws more pumpkin pranks!

Green Goblin flies away.
Spidey cannot reach him.

Ms. Marvel cannot
reach him, either!

Green Goblin wants
to spread more Giggle Gas.

Spidey and Ms. Marvel
must stop him!

Ms. Marvel stretches
to send Spidey flying!

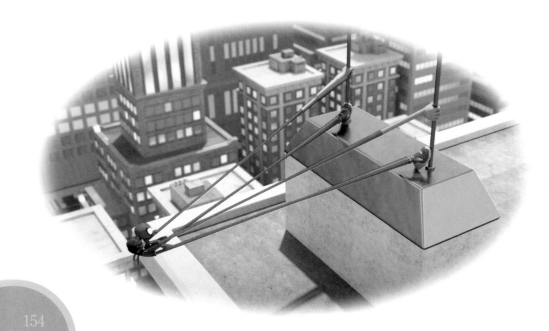

Spidey surprises
Green Goblin.

Spidey thwips his webs.
He stops the Giggle Gas.

Green Goblin gets a taste
of his own Giggle Gas.
He starts to laugh!

Green Goblin falls right into
Ms. Marvel's big hands.

Spidey takes the loot
from the store.

Spidey and Ms. Marvel
saved the day!

Spidey webs up
Green Goblin.
Way to go, Spidey
and Ms. Marvel!